The Buddy Files

THE CASE OF THE
FIRE
ALARM

Dori Hillestad Butler
Pictures by Jeremy Tugeau

Albert Whitman & Company
Chicago, Illinois

Library of Congress Cataloging-in-Publication Data

Butler, Dori Hillestad.

The Buddy files : the case of the fire alarm / by Dori Hillestad Butler;
pictures by Jeremy Tugeau.

p. cm.

Summary: When Buddy goes to school to become a therapy dog, he ends up helping
figure out who pulled the fire alarm instead.

ISBN 978-0-8075-0913-5 (hc)
ISBN 978-0-8075-0935-7 (sc)
[1. Dogs–Fiction. 2. Schools–Fiction. 3. Mystery and detective stories.]
I. Tugeau, Jeremy, ill. II. Title. III. Title: Case of the fire alarm.

PZ7.B9759Bt 2010

[Fic]–dc22

2010004326

The design is by Nick Tiemersma.

For more information about Albert Whitman & Company,
please visit our web site at www.albertwhitman.com.

For the Nano Rebels,
the best friends a writer
or dog could ever have!

Table of Contents

1
Starting School

Hello!

My name is Buddy.

I used to be a detective. I used to solve mysteries with my old human, Kayla. But Kayla moved to Springtown, and now I have new humans. Their names are Connor and Mom.

I'm giving up the detective business because I have a new job to think about.

I'm going to be a THERAPY DOG!
That means I'm going to sit, lie down,
stay, and come when I'm called. I'll
walk nicely next to Mom, and I won't
pick up treats on the floor unless
someone says I can. I won't even speak
to other dogs. And I'll make friends
with lots and lots and lots of humans.

I also get to ride IN THE CAR
every time I go to my job. In fact, I am
IN THE CAR right now. I LOVE the
car. It's my favorite thing!

And I'm sitting next to Connor. I
LOVE Connor. He's my favorite boy!

"Ew! Buddy!" Connor says, wiping
his face. "No lick!"

Connor, Mom, and I are all on our
way to SCHOOL. I LOVE school. It's
my favorite place! It's where Connor

and Mom go every day. And now *I* get to go there every day, too, because that's where my new job is.

Except... the car is stopping and we are not at school. We're at Mouse's house. Why are we stopping at Mouse's house?

I stick my head out the window. "Mouse!" I call. "Hey, Mouse! Are you coming to school with us?"

Mouse is my friend. He's a dog, not a mouse. In fact, he's the biggest, loudest dog on our street. Hey, maybe he's going to be a therapy dog, too!

Mouse pokes his head out of his doghouse. "NO, I'M NOT GOING TO SCHOOL," he says. It sounds like he's yelling, but he's not. He talks this loud all the time. "THERE'S A

NEW BOY AT MY HOUSE. HE'S THE
ONE WHO'S GOING TO SCHOOL.
NOT ME."

"You have a new boy?" I say.

"YES. MY HUMANS JUST
BROUGHT HIM HOME YESTER-
DAY."

Mouse's humans bring home new
boys and girls a lot. I don't know where
they get them all. Most of the kids are
nice, but the last one they had threw
rocks at Mouse.

"Is this a nice boy?" I ask nervously.

"OF COURSE HE'S A NICE BOY,"
Mouse says.

I think Mouse forgot about the kid
who threw rocks.

I see Mouse's new boy, but I can't
smell him yet. He's walking toward

our car with Jack. Jack is the alpha human at Mouse's house. He smells like cars and gasoline.

The boy is about Connor's size, and he has long, shaggy hair. There's something shiny in his right earlobe.

Mom rolls down her window when he and Jack get close.

"Good morning, Sarah," Jack says to Mom. "This is our new foster son, Michael."

"Nice to meet you, Michael," Mom says. She tilts her head toward the backseat. "This is my son, Connor. I think you two are in the same grade."

Jack opens the back door, and Michael climbs in next to me.

"Hey," Connor says.

Michael just grunts.

I sniff Michael all over. He smells like peanut butter toast and dirt and ... I'm not sure what else. I hope he's not another rock thrower.

Mom waves goodbye to Jack and backs out of their driveway.

"So," Connor says to Michael, "where are you from?"

"Minneapolis," Michael says, gazing out the window.

"I'm from Los Angeles," Connor says. "I just moved here, too. My mom and dad got divorced, and my dad is still in California."

Michael doesn't say anything to that, so Connor asks another question. "What do you like to do?"

Michael shrugs.

"Do you play baseball?" Connor

asks. "Basketball? Soccer?"

Michael shrugs again. I don't think he's much of a talker.

Connor keeps trying. "What about music? Do you play an instrument? Do you like to read? Do art? Play computer games?"

"I like ghost stories," Michael says finally. "Books ... movies ... anything with ghosts in it."

"Yeah?" Connor says. "Then you'll like our school. We've got a ghost!"

A ghost?

"Connor!" Mom makes why-would-you-say-such-a-thing eyes at Connor in the rearview mirror.

"What?" he says. "It's true. There was a fire at our school a long time ago, and part of the school burned down. This girl—her name was Agatha Curry—she got burned up in the fire, and now her ghost haunts the old part of the school."

Mom shakes her head. "That's just a story, Connor," she says. "It's not true."

"Yes, it is," Connor insists. "Kids have seen her, Mom. So has the janitor."

"Mr. Poe likes to tell stories," Mom says. "And he likes to get kids all riled up. There's no such thing as a ghost, Connor. You know that."

I didn't *think* there was any such thing as a ghost. But I'm glad to hear Mom say it.

We pull into the school parking lot, and Mom parks the car. I see kids playing on the swings ... kids playing chase—I LOVE chase. It's my favorite game! Oh, and over there I see kids hitting a ball around a pole. That looks even better than chase!

"Let me out!" I say, scratching at the door. "I want to PLAY BALL!"

Mom opens the door, and Connor hands her my leash.

"Is that our new therapy dog?" a girl about Connor's age calls out. She and a bunch of other kids run toward us.

Oh, boy! New friends. I LOVE new friends!

"Yes, this is Buddy," Mom says.

I am trying to sniff and lick all these kids, but there are too many of them. And they are all petting me!

I LOVE getting petted!
   "I need to take Buddy inside now,"
Mom says as she tries to lead me away.

Aw ... so soon?
"Bye, Buddy," Connor says. He and Michael race toward that pole with the ball.

"Where are you taking him? Where is he going to be?" a boy with a missing tooth asks.

"He'll be in my office most of the time," Mom says. "But once he settles in, Mrs. Warner will have him in the library sometimes, too. You'll be able to sign up for reading sessions with him."

"Yay!" the kids cheer.

Mom opens the door to the school. "This way, Buddy," she says, guiding me down the hall. My toes make a funny clicking sound as we walk. Just like at the vet's office.

There are so many interesting smells in this place. Pancakes... sausage... I LOVE pancakes and sausage. They're my favorite foods!

I also smell shoes. Lots of shoes. And dirt. And perfume. And coffee. I think we are moving closer to the coffee. And farther away from the pancakes and sausage. Too bad!

Mom leads me into a room with a desk and table, plants, and lots of windows. There are two ladies in here. One of them is sitting at the desk. She's an older lady with curly hair, and she smells very nice. Like liver treats. I LOVE liver treats. They're my favorite food!

"Ellie," Mom says to the lady, "this is Buddy."

Ellie smiles at me. "Hi, Buddy."

I rest my chin on Ellie's desk. She reaches into her pocket and pulls out a LIVER TREAT! She hands the treat to me, and I gobble it up. Mmm. I think Ellie and I are going to be good friends.

I'm not so sure about the other lady. She smells like hot pepper and pineapple, and she's looking at me like *I'm* the one who smells bad.

"I can't believe the school board approved this," the hot-pepper-and-pineapple lady tells Mom. "Dogs don't belong in schools."

"Buddy is well trained, Mrs. Argus," Mom says, scratching my ears. "And I think there's a lot of good that can come from having a dog at school. Studies have shown that simply petting a dog lowers heart rate and blood pressure—"

"Yes, I read the information you

passed around," Mrs. Argus says. "But that doesn't mean I agree with it. I'll be watching this dog." She points a finger at me. "One wrong move, and he's out of here!"

2
Trouble

One wrong move? What does *that* mean?

"Don't worry, Sarah," Ellie tells Mom after Mrs. Argus leaves. "Mona is slow to warm up to new ideas. But she'll come around. In time."

"I hope so," Mom says. She brings me into a smaller room across from Ellie's desk, then takes off my leash. There's a desk and chair in the middle of the room, two chairs on the other side of the desk, a big fluffy pillow under the window, and a water bowl next to the pillow.

Everything in here smells like Mom. This must be where she works. And when Mom points to the pillow, I know this is where I'll be working, too.

I turn two circles on the pillow, then plop down and wait for Mom to tell me what to do next. Does she want me to sit? Will she throw a piece of hot dog on the floor and tell me to leave it? What does she want me to do?

I watch as Mom sits down at her desk, turns on the computer, and starts writing on some papers.

I let out a small woof, in case she's forgotten I'm here.

"What's the matter, Buddy?" Mom asks. "Do you need to go outside?"

"No," I tell Mom with my eyes. I just want to know what I'm supposed to do. *I don't want to make a wrong move.*

"You were just outside before we got here," Mom says. "You shouldn't need to go outside already."

I already said I don't need to go outside.

"You just lie there and be a good dog," Mom says.

That's it? That's all you want me to do? Lie here and be a good dog? I can do that!

I rest my head on my paws and

let my eyes close. I think about how much I like my new job already. I'm not going to get into any trouble while I'm here. I'm going to make new friends. Maybe I'll even make friends with Mrs. Argus. That would be nice...

Then I hear a strange, almost ghostly voice. "He-e-el-l-l-p me, Buddy."

Huh? Who said that?

I look around. I'm not in the office anymore. I'm in a big room with lots and lots of books. And right behind me is a girl with a burned face. But she's not a real girl. She's like a...ghost girl. I can see right through her.

She reaches for me. "He-e-el-l-l-p

me, Buddy," she says again.

I step back. "H-how do you know my name?" I ask. She scares me. You're not supposed to be able to see through humans.

"Mom?" a voice interrupts. "Can Buddy come outside to play during recess?"

Connor?

My eyes pop open. The ghost girl and the room with the books disappear. *It was all just a dream.*

I'm still here in the office. With Mom. And Connor wants to take me outside to play.

I sit up and give myself a good shake. I would really like to go outside to play.

"Sure," Mom says. "He could use

some exercise."

"Let's go!" I tell Connor, wagging my tail. I'm already at the door.

Connor grabs my leash. "Does Buddy have to have his leash on outside?" he asks.

"Of course," Mom says.

Connor groans. "Why? I won't take him on the blacktop. We'll stay on the other playground. The one that's fenced."

"I don't want anyone to feel scared if there's a dog running around loose on the playground," Mom says.

"Who would be scared?" Connor asks. "Buddy's a good dog. And I told everyone that we could play fetch with him. How can he fetch on a leash?"

Mom thinks about this. "Well," she says after a little while. "I suppose we could try having him off-leash on the back playground."

"Yes!" Connor cries.

"But keep the leash on until you're outside," Mom says. "And if he starts to bother anyone, put the leash back on right away."

"Okay," Connor says.

We head down the hall... down the stairs... around the corner... and out onto the playground, where there are kids running and balls flying EVERYWHERE!

Connor unhooks my leash, and I RUN! I love to run! I love to chase! I LOVE to play ball! It's my favorite thing!

If that's not exciting enough,
there are new friends all around me.
Real friends, not ghost friends. And
everyone is trying to get my attention.
"Come here, Dog!" "Here, boy! Here,
boy!" "He looks just like my friend
Kayla's dog!"

Wait. Who said that last thing?
I look all around me. It sounded like
Kayla's friend, Jillian.

It IS Jillian! "Hey, Jillian!" I cry,
barreling toward her. "How are you
doing?"

But before I get to her, another kid
calls, "Come here, Dog!"

"His name's Buddy, not Dog,"
Connor says.

"Come here, Buddy!" "Does he play
ball?" "Hey, Buddy! Go fetch!"

Whoa! There goes another ball! I run after it...

"No, come here, Buddy!" Jillian calls me.

I stop. I don't know where to go or what to do or who to play with. I'm standing next to a kid who is smaller than Connor. He smells like bananas, sweat socks, and dirt. In fact, there's a little piece of banana stuck to his shirt. I LOVE bananas. They're my favorite food!

I'll just clean that banana off his shirt. His alpha human will never know it was there.

"If you want to join the Sharks, you have to do something no one else at our school has ever done. Something to prove you're worthy," the kid says as he pushes me away.

"Yeah, we don't let just anyone into our club," says another kid, who smells like hamburger, pencils, and dirt.

Huh? What are these kids talking about? Oh, they're not talking to me. They're talking to that *really* little kid over there. The one that smells like blueberry muffins.

"I can jump higher than anyone in my class," Blueberry Muffin Kid says. He jumps up to a high bar on the climbing toy to prove it.

The two bigger kids laugh. "You think no one else in the whole school can jump up to that bar?"

"Hey, Buddy?" a dog calls behind me. "Is that you?"

I whirl around again. There's a
pug on the other side of the far fence.
I know that pug!

"Jazzy!" I say.

Jazzy wags her tail. "You remember
me?"

"Of course I remember you," I
say, running toward her. I just met
her twelve ... or three ... or eleventy-
three days ago. She got mixed up with
another dog that kind of looked like
her, but didn't smell anything like her.
I solved the mystery and got both dogs
back where they belonged.

"Come back, Buddy," Connor calls,
waving a ball at me.

"Yeah, play with us!" some other
kids holler.

Hmm. I want to play ... and I want

33

to talk to Jazzy ... and I want to
make new friends ... and ... I don't
know what I want most!

"It's okay," Jazzy says. "Go play!
We'll talk later."

"Okay, see you later!" I turn
and—BANG! I accidentally run right
into Blueberry Muffin Kid. He falls
to the ground.

"Oops. Sorry," I say.

I sniff him to see if he's hurt. There isn't any water coming out of his eyes, but there's red stuff coming out of his arm. I remember when Kayla fell off her bike and there was red stuff on her knee. Red stuff is bad.

Two girls rush over. "Are you okay, Zack?" one asks.

"You're bleeding. You need to go to the nurse," says the other girl.

"What's going on over there?" a teacher calls.

Uh-oh. It's Mrs. Argus. The lady who said, "One wrong move…"

Mrs. Argus puts her hands on her hips. "Did that dog knock you down, Zack?" she asks Blueberry Muffin Kid.

"Sort of," Zack says, rubbing his elbow.

Mrs. Argus makes angry noises through her nose and grabs me by the collar. "Would you two walk Zack to the nurse's office?" she asks the girls.

They both nod. Each one reaches a hand out to Zack and pulls him up.

Mrs. Argus drags me toward the school.

"Hey!" Connor calls, running up

behind us. "Where are you going with my dog?" My leash is dangling from his fingers.

Mrs. Argus snatches the leash from Connor, but doesn't put it on me.

"We're going to see your mother," she tells Connor.

I swallow hard.

We go into the school ... up the stairs ... around the corner ... down the hall ... into Ellie's office and then into Mom's office. Mom is sitting at her desk.

My tail droops. I can't even look at Mom.

"I told you dogs don't belong in school," Mrs. Argus tells Mom. She drops my leash on the floor, but keeps a very tight hold on my collar. "Your dog just attacked one of my first-graders!"

"Attacked?" Mom and I say at the same time.

I step forward. "No! It was an accident!" I explain. "I didn't attack anyone—"

"I don't know what happened outside, but I assure you, Mrs. Argus, Buddy would *never* attack anyone," Mom says.

"Well, he just knocked Zack Goodman completely off his feet. Zack is in the nurse's office right now. I warned you—"

"Sarah? Would you like me to check on Zack?" Ellie asks from the outer office. She has a telephone in her hand.

"Yes, please," Mom says wearily. She rubs her forehead.

"I'm going to report this to the superintendent," Mrs. Argus tells Mom. "And then I'm going to call Zack's parents. We'll see how *they* feel about having a dog in this school."

With that, Mrs. Argus lets go of my collar and storms out of the office.

Mom looks at me.

"I didn't attack him," I say again. Then I lie down on my pillow and make myself as small as I can. *I'm not a bad dog. Really, I'm not.*

Ellie comes into Mom's office. "It's okay," she says to Mom. She bends down and gives my ears a scratch. "The nurse said it was just a little scrape. Zack is fine. He said Buddy didn't mean to knock him down. He's on his way back to his classroom."

"Thank goodness," Mom says, leaning back in her chair. "You know, we had a therapy dog at my old school. It was such a positive experience. Kids read to him. He helped with peer conflict. Everyone loved him. I had no idea people here wouldn't be in favor of the idea."

"Most people are in favor of it," Ellie assures Mom. "It's just—"

Ellie's words are cut off by a noise so loud and so horrible I feel like my head is about to explode.

3
Fire!

"STOP!" I howl. "Make that
horrible noise STOP!"

Mom gets up from her desk and
snaps the leash to my collar. Then
she brings me out into the hallway.
The noise is even louder out here.

Classroom doors swing open.
Kids and teachers pour out of all the
rooms, but no one is stopping that
noise.

"I DIDN'T KNOW THERE WAS GOING TO BE A FIRE DRILL TODAY!" one of the teachers says loudly.

"THERE WASN'T ONE SCHEDULED!" Mom replies.

"THEN WHY IS THE FIRE ALARM GOING OFF?" a girl asks. "IS THE SCHOOL ON FIRE?"

Fire? Sniff... sniff... I don't think the school is on fire. I don't smell smoke. But it's hard to concentrate on my nose with all that NOISE pounding through my head.

Mom hands my leash to Ellie. "Would you take Buddy outside, please?"

"Sure," Ellie says. She leads me into the sea of humans moving down the hall. We walk beside kids who are yelling, "FIRE! FIRE!"... down the stairs... around the corner... and out the door.

Oh, much better! It's quieter out here. But my ears are still ringing.

Ellie and I walk all the way to the fence. I see Jazzy sitting in her yard on the other side of the fence. She is watching everyone come out of school.

"Do you hear that noise?" I ask Jazzy.

"Yes," she says, like it's no big deal. "It's just a fire drill."

Fire drill? "What's a fire drill?" I ask. I heard people in the school say those words. But Mom said there *wasn't* a fire drill scheduled for today.

"A fire drill is when humans

pretend there's a fire—" Jazzy stops. "What's that?" She tilts her head.

It sounds like sirens. They're coming closer. And closer. I hear a loud horn beep, then I see flashing lights.

"Is that a fire truck?" I ask, stretching my neck. Why would a fire truck come if this is just pretend? I make my way through the crowd of kids to get a closer look.

"Slow down, Buddy," Ellie says,
holding tight to my leash.

It's not just one fire truck. It's
one ... nine ... seven fire trucks. And
one ... four police cars. They are all
driving around to the front of the
school.

Is the school on fire?

I can't get to where the fire trucks are because there's another fence in the way. But the door to the school is standing wide open. I make a run for it.

"BUDDY!" Ellie cries as I yank the leash out of her hand.

Oops. I didn't mean to pull the leash … but maybe it's good that I did. If the school is on fire, I don't want to put Ellie in any danger. "You stay here," I tell her. "I'm just going to check things out."

I race toward the school, then skid to a stop. That horrible NOISE is still sounding inside the building. Do I really want to go back in there? I could just let the firefighters handle the problem.

No. I'm better at sniffing out trouble than most humans are. If there's a fire, I'll find it. And if there are humans trapped in the school, I'll find them, too.

I head for the door, but a man who smells like cleaning stuff stops me. "You stay out here, boy," he says to me.

"But...but..." I sputter. "I can help."

"No one goes back inside until the all clear is given," the man says. "That includes dogs."

Fine.

I run along the outside of the school. Sniffing...sniffing...sniffing. I still don't smell fire. I don't even smell smoke.

So why did the fire trucks come if there's no fire? And why did that terrible noise go off if no fire drill was scheduled?

I'm kind of worried about all of this. It would help if someone I knew gave me a little pat or told me I was a good dog.

I look around. I don't see Connor or Ellie in the crowd. But I do see my old friend Jillian. She is standing off to the side with a girl I don't know.

I go over and nudge Jillian's hand to get her to pet me. But Jillian is too busy talking to her friend to give me any attention.

"Are you sure no one saw you?" the friend whispers. She smells like honey and cinnamon.

"I'm sure," Jillian whispers back. "I saw a kid go into the boys' bathroom, but he didn't see me. No one saw me."

A school bell rings, and everyone starts moving quickly toward the building.

I hear Ellie calling, "Buddy? Come here, Buddy!"

Ah, there you are, Ellie! I run to her. She picks up my leash, and we head for school.

No one is blocking the door anymore. And that terrible NOISE inside the school has finally stopped.

"Was there really a fire?" a boy asks.

"I don't think so," says one of the teachers.

"Then why did the fire alarm go off?" a girl asks.

No one answers her.

The kids all go back to their classrooms, and Ellie and I go back into the office. Mom is already in there. She's talking to a firefighter who is wearing a heavy coat, boots, and pants that all smell like smoke, fire, and mud. But he didn't pick up the smoke, fire, and mud here.

"There's no fire," the firefighter tells Mom. His jaw is set tight. "I think one of your kids pulled the fire alarm."

4
Clues

Mom has my leash tied around her belt. It isn't very tight.

We follow the firefighter down the hall and around the corner, my nose to the ground. I smell people. LOTS of people have walked down this hallway. I also smell paint … and glue … and books … and crackers and cheese. Oh, I LOVE crackers and cheese. They're my favorite foods!

The crackers and cheese smell is coming from that room over there. I pull toward that room, and the leash slips away from Mom's belt.

Wow! What a great classroom *this* is. Little kids are sitting at their desks, munching on crackers and cheese. I wonder if five or nine of those kids would share their crackers and cheese with me...

"Look! There's Buddy! Hi, Buddy!" the kids say when I walk in.

The girl closest to the door offers me her cracker. "Hey, thanks!" I say, gobbling it up.

The next kid hasn't even started eating his crackers and cheese. "If you don't want your crackers and cheese, I'll take them," I offer.

Oh! It's Blueberry Muffin Kid, otherwise known as Zack. The kid I accidentally knocked down outside. I guess he's still mad about that because he's not going to share his food with me.

"Hey!" says a sharp voice. I hear hands clapping, and I look up.

It's Mrs. Argus. *Why do I keep running into her?*

"I'm sorry, Mrs. Argus," Mom says right behind me. She grabs my leash.

Mrs. Argus clicks her tongue. "First your dog knocked one of my students down. Now he's running around loose, stealing food from my first-graders."

What? No, I'm not!

"I promise this won't happen again," Mom says as she leads me out of the room.

"But ... I didn't steal anything," I say. "I'm being a good dog! Really, I am."

"Bye, Buddy! See you later, Buddy!" the kids say.

I wag my tail at them, then go down the hall with Mom and the firefighter.

"This is the alarm that was pulled." The firefighter points at a small red box on the wall. It's up pretty high. Too high for me to sniff without getting up on my hind legs. That's okay. If that's the thing that made the terrible noise, I don't need to sniff it. I want to stay as far away from it as I can.

"I can't imagine who would have pulled the alarm," Mom says, rubbing her chin.

The firefighter glances at me. "Your dog looks like he wants to help us find out who did it," he says with a smile.

"Oh, no," I say. I'm about to tell the firefighter that I'm a therapy dog now. I don't solve mysteries anymore.

But then I remember Mrs. Argus. She thinks I'm a bad dog. She thinks I attacked one of her students. And now she thinks I'm a thief, too! I need to do something to show her I'm not a bad dog.

Maybe I *should* help Mom and the firefighter find out who pulled the alarm. Then Mrs. Argus will see what a GOOD DOG I am, and she won't try to get me kicked out of the school.

I get right to work. Sniff... sniff... sniff. My nose is my best tool for crime-solving.

Whoever pulled this alarm must have left a trail. All we have to do is find it... and follow it.

Here it is! "Follow me, guys," I say.

Wait. There's another trail over here. And another one over here. And another one over here. And another one over here!

This isn't going to work. There are too many trails. Too many people have walked down this hallway.

How else can I solve this mystery? Are there any other clues?

I see some mud on the floor.

There's mud by the fire alarm and all along the hallway. *Could that be a clue?*

I don't want to get too close to that alarm box, but I have to see if there are any clues up there. I get up on my hind legs and sniff.

Paint? Is that paint on the alarm? That's what it smells like. I think the color of that paint is called green.

Mom pulls me down.

"Yeah, but do you see the paint on the alarm?" I say. I hop back up on my hind legs to show her the paint, but she pulls me down again.

"You should talk to the teachers who have classes in this hallway," the firefighter says. "See if any of them saw anything."

Mom nods. "I'll also find out if any of their students had a bathroom pass about the time the alarm went off." She points at the two closed doors across the hall. "Someone in the bathroom could have seen or heard something."

I paw at Mom's leg. "Ask the teachers if their kids were painting this morning, too," I say.

"Buddy, shh!" Mom says.

"A kid in the bathroom may have seen something," the firefighter says. "But if he was away from the rest of his class, he could have been the one who *pulled* the alarm."

Wow, that's a smart firefighter!

"Are you guys writing this stuff down?" I ask Mom. "We should make lists of things we know, things we don't know, and things we can do to find out what we don't know." That's what a good detective does.

Here is what we know about this case:

- 🐾 The fire alarm went off.
- 🐾 Fire alarms are LOUD!!!
- 🐾 Somebody pulled the alarm on purpose.
- 🐾 There is mud in the hallway by the alarm.
- 🐾 There is green paint on the alarm.

Here is what we don't know:

- 🐾 Who pulled the fire alarm???

Here are some things we can do
to find out who pulled the fire alarm:

- 🐾 Find out which kids were painting this morning.
- 🐾 Find out whether any of the teachers saw anything.
- 🐾 Find out if anyone was in the bathroom. That person may have seen something OR that person may be a suspect!

"So, who's going to do what?" I
ask. I look at Mom. Then I look at the
firefighter.

Neither of them volunteers to do
anything.

"How about I sniff around and
see if I can find out which kids were

painting this morning," I offer, just to get things moving. We aren't going to solve this case by standing around.

"Hey, what's this?" Mom peers closer at the alarm box. She presses her finger against the smudge of paint, then looks at her finger with surprise. "Paint?" she says.

Yes, it's paint. I showed you that eleventy-twelve minutes ago!

My ears twitch. I hear footsteps.

I watch the hallway to see who's coming. Oh, it's Ellie! I wag my tail.

"There you are, Sarah," she says. "There's a phone call for you in the office."

Mom turns. "Can you take a message, please? We're in the middle of something here."

"Sure," Ellie nods.

"And would you take Buddy with you?" Mom asks. "He's getting in the way."

Getting in the way?

"I'd be happy to," Ellie says, reaching for my leash. "Come on, Buddy."

I don't want to go with Ellie. I want to stay and solve the Case of the Fire Alarm. "Please can't I stay?" I ask Mom.

Mom turns to the firefighter, and they start talking in hushed voices. But no one understands what I am saying. I have no choice but to follow Ellie back to the office.

5
Telling Lies

It's not fair! I could help Mom and the firefighter. I could find clues that they miss. If they'd let me.

When Ellie and I get back to the office, I go right to my pillow, turn a circle, and plop down. I wonder how Mom and the firefighter are doing. Did they talk to any teachers? Did they find out whether anyone was in the bathroom? Did they find out which kids were painting this morning? And what about the mud on the floor? Did they ever even notice that?

Mom comes back a little while later.

I sit up. "Well?" I say.

She doesn't offer any information. She just closes her door, sits down at her desk, and starts writing something on a piece of paper.

I get up and walk over to her. I wish I could read what she was writing on that paper. But I don't know how to read.

"Hey, Buddy," she says, patting my side. "How are you doing?"

"I'm okay," I tell her with my eyes. "Did you solve the case? Do you know who pulled the fire alarm?"

Before Mom can answer, there's a knock on her door. Ellie pokes her head into the room. "You wanted to see these three?" she says.

"Yes," Mom says. She motions for them to come in.

Hey, I know these kids. I know *all* of these kids. First there's Michael, who is Mouse's new human. Then Jillian, who is Kayla's old friend. And finally, Zack, the kid I accidentally knocked down outside.

They all walk very slowly into Mom's office. I smell FEAR on all three of them. Lots of fear, which is strange because Mom is so nice! Why would anyone be afraid to come and visit her?

Ellie brings an extra chair
from the main office and sets it
beside the other two in front of
Mom's desk.

"Sit down," Mom says.

Michael, Jillian, and Zack all sit.
Ellie closes the door on her way out.

"You're probably wondering
why I called you down here," Mom
begins. "It's about the fire alarm.
Somebody pulled it. On purpose."

Mom waits, but no one says anything.

"Did you know that it's a crime
to pull a fire alarm when there's no
fire?" Mom asks. "What if there had
been a real fire across town when
the firefighters were busy with our
false alarm?"

Still nothing from Michael, Jillian, or Zack.

"You three weren't in your class-rooms when the alarm went off," Mom says. "In fact, you were all somewhere near the alarm. Do any of you know

who pulled it?"

Michael and Jillian glance at each other. Zack looks down at the floor.

Hmm. Michael and Zack both have mud on their shoes. Jillian *doesn't* have mud on her shoes.

Could either of those boys have pulled the alarm? I go over and sniff them. I don't really smell anything interesting on either one of them.

I *do* smell something interesting on Jillian, though. Paint.

Where is it? Where's the paint? While Jillian scratches my ears, I sniff, sniff, sniff the bottom of her leg...her lap...her hand. Ah, there it is! On her hands. *It's the same color as the paint on the alarm.*

But that doesn't mean Jillian pulled the alarm. Jillian was Kayla's friend. She's a nice girl. She would never commit a crime.

"Your class was in the library when the alarm went off," Mom says to Jillian. "But your teacher says you had a bathroom pass."

"Yes," Jillian says softly.

Michael's mouth drops open. "That girl didn't go into the bathroom!" he says. "She went into that other room across the hall."

"What other room?" Mom asks. "The art room?"

"I don't know," Michael says. "Whatever room is next to the alarm. She went in there right before the alarm went off. I could tell she was up to something. She kept looking over her shoulder like she didn't want anyone to see her. I don't think anyone else was in that other room."

"I was in the bathroom," Jillian insists. "I was in the bathroom the whole time."

My stomach tightens. *Jillian is not telling the truth!*

It's hard to explain how I know that. But you can see a lie in a human's eyes, mouth, and in the way they hold their bodies. Sometimes you can even smell it on them.

Mom turns to Michael. "What were *you* doing in the hallway?" she asks. "The rest of your class was outside when the alarm went off."

"I had to go to the bathroom," Michael says.

"Did you have a bathroom pass?" Mom asks.

Michael pauses. "No," he says.

"Why not?"

"I didn't know I needed one."

Mom frowns at him. "In this school,

you always need permission when you leave the rest of your class."

"Fine," Michael says, slouching down in his seat.

Mom turns back to Jillian. "I see you've got some paint on your hands."

Jillian quickly slides her hands under her legs.

"It looks like green paint," Mom says. "Did you know there was some green paint on the fire alarm?"

"A lot of kids in Mrs. Doyle's room have green paint on their hands," Jillian says in a small voice. "We had art this morning. We were painting vegetables."

"Aren't you in Mrs. Doyle's room, too?" Mom asks Michael. "Do you have paint on your hands?"

Michael holds up clean hands. "I did, but I washed it off," he says. "When I went to the bathroom."

I don't know ... there's something about Michael. I wouldn't say he's exactly lying ... but something about him doesn't smell right. It's like he's hiding something.

Mom turns to Zack. "You're the one who got knocked down on the playground, aren't you?" she says. "That's why you weren't in your classroom. You were on your way back to your class from the nurse's office."

Zack is so scared when Mom talks to him that his whole body trembles.

Mom softens her voice. "Another teacher says you stopped to help her hang up a mural in the hallway before you got back to your class. Is that right?"

Zack nods once.

"She also said you got some paint on your hand, so she told you to go to the bathroom to wash up. That's where you were headed when the alarm went off."

Zack had paint on his hand, too?

"I don't think you're tall enough to pull the fire alarm," Mom says right away. "But did you see either of these two pull it?"

Zack doesn't look at Michael or Jillian. He just shakes his head quickly.

I can't tell whether he's telling the truth or not. I can't see his face. And the only thing I can smell on him is FEAR. I don't blame him for being afraid. He's younger than those other kids. If he did see either of them pull the alarm, he's not going to want to say so.

Finally, Michael jumps to his feet. "I know you think I did it. But just because I pulled the fire alarm at my old school doesn't mean I pulled it here!"

Michael pulled the fire alarm at his old school?

Mom raises an eyebrow. "You pulled the fire alarm at your old school?"

"Y-you didn't know that?" Michael asks.

"No, actually, I didn't," Mom says. But she seems very interested in this information.

I'm interested, too. Michael is tall enough to pull the alarm. He admitted he had paint on his hands, but he washed it off. And he has pulled a fire alarm before.

"I didn't pull it!" Michael says.

"Neither did I!" Jillian says.

"Neither did I," Zack whispers.

I smell another lie. But this time I'm not sure who it's coming from.

"I don't know who pulled the fire alarm," Mom says. "But I will find out. And when I do..."

I gulp. I didn't pull the alarm, but when Mom uses that tone of voice, I feel scared anyway, for the person who did.

6
Late Night Secrets

It's dark in Connor's room. I'm snuggled up against Connor on his bed, and I'm thinking about the Case of the Fire Alarm.

Here is what I know about Zack:

- 🐾 He had mud on his shoes.
- 🐾 A teacher sent him to the bathroom because he had paint on his hand.

* He is too short to pull the fire alarm.

Here is what I know about Michael:
* He had mud on his shoes.
* He had paint on his hands, but he washed it off.
* His class was outside when the alarm was pulled, but he came inside to use the bathroom.
* He did not have a bathroom pass.
* He pulled the fire alarm at his old school.

Here is what I know about Jillian:

- 🐾 She did not have mud on her shoes.
- 🐾 She had paint on her hand.
- 🐾 She was seen coming out of the art room.
- 🐾 Jillian says she wasn't in the art room, but that is a lie.
- 🐾 Wherever Jillian was, she had permission to leave her class.
- 🐾 Jillian was Kayla's friend, and she would NEVER, EVER, EVER pull a fire alarm.

I don't think the mud is going to help me solve this case. Lots of people have mud on their shoes. That mud could have been left by anyone who walked down that hallway.

The paint isn't going to help me, either. Lots of kids were painting this morning.

So what do I know that will help me solve this case?

I go over everything I know about Zach, Michael, and Jillian inside my head again.

Hmmm...

Okay, maybe I shouldn't say Jillian would never, ever, ever pull a fire alarm. I know it, but I shouldn't say it because it's an opinion. An opinion is when you THINK something is true, but you have no proof that it's true.

Uh-oh.

I just thought of one more thing I know about Jillian:

🐾 **When everyone was outside after the alarm went off, she told her friend, "No one saw me."**

No one saw her do what? I wonder. *Pull the fire alarm?*

No! She had to have been talking about something else.

I think Michael pulled the alarm. But I don't have proof of that, either.

Hey, Michael lives at Mouse's house. Maybe if I go over to Mouse's house, I could *find* proof that Michael pulled the alarm. Maybe Mouse will even help me find proof.

That sounds like a Plan!

I carefully step over Connor and jump down from the bed. Connor rolls over, but doesn't wake up. Out in the hallway, I pause to listen at Mom's door. I hear snoring. Good! I continue down the stairs, through the kitchen, and out the doggy door.

"Mouse!" I call. "Hey, Mouse. Are you awake? I'm coming over!"

"YOU ARE?" Mouse says. "YAY!!!"

Except... I'm not sure how I'm going to get there.

There *used to be* a secret tunnel that went from my yard, under the fence, and into the Deerbergs' yard. But Mom and Connor found the tunnel and filled it in.

I guess I could dig a new tunnel.

I pick a different spot along the
fence. I hope this place is better
hidden. And I start digging.

"I THOUGHT YOU WERE
COMING OVER *NOW*," Mouse says
after a little while.

"I am!" I say from halfway under
the fence. "I just have to ... finish ...
this ... tunnel!" There! I'm through! I
scramble up out of the hole and across
the Deerbergs' yard.

Unfortunately, there's another
fence between the Deerbergs' yard
and Mouse's yard. But it's shorter
than my fence. Maybe I can climb over
it. I take a running jump. I am up ...
and over!

"THERE YOU ARE!" Mouse
says as we greet each other the dog-

fashioned way. "WHAT WAS SO IMPORTANT THAT YOU HAD TO COME OVER?"

I tell Mouse about the fire alarm and who I think pulled it.

He growls at me.

"What?" I say.

"I DON'T LIKE YOU TALKING BAD ABOUT MY BOY."

Mouse thinks Michael is "his boy"? Already?

"Well, Michael has pulled a fire alarm before," I tell Mouse. In fact, I tell Mouse everything I know about Michael, Jillian, and Zack.

"NONE OF THAT MEANS *MICHAEL* PULLED THE ALARM!" Mouse says.

"Well," I say. "I don't think Jillian

did it. And Zack is too short. Who else could have done it?"

"SOMEBODY WHO IS NOT MICHAEL!!!" Mouse says. This time he's showing teeth.

"Okay, okay," I say, backing down.

Maybe I should just go home. Mouse isn't going to help me find proof that Michael pulled the alarm. And I don't want to get into a fight with him.

I start toward the fence. But a shuffling in the pile of firewood at the back of Mouse's yard stops me in my tracks. A single log shifts and falls onto the lawn.

I freeze. *Someone is back there.*

"Hello?" I say, peering into the darkness. But I don't see anyone.

Mouse comes to stand beside me.
"WHO'S THERE?" he barks. "SHOW
YOURSELF!"

A shadowy figure with pointy
ears slo-o-w-l-y climbs to the top of the
woodpile.

It's Cat with No Name! "What
makes you dogs so sure a *human*
pulled that alarm at the school?"
Cat asks.

Mouse and I look at each other.
What is that cat talking about?

"*I* didn't pull it," I say. "And Mouse
didn't pull it."

Then it hits me. "Did *you* pull it?"
I ask Cat.

Cat with No Name looks at me like
I'm an idiot. "No!" he says, blinking
his eyes.

"Well, what other nonhuman could have pulled it?" I ask.

"Duh! How about the *ghost* of Four Lakes Elementary?" Cat says.

"THERE'S NO SUCH THING AS GHOSTS," Mouse says. "IS THERE, BUDDY?"

"Of course not," I say. How dumb does Cat think Mouse and I are?

"Just because you dogs can't *see* ghosts doesn't mean they're not there," Cat says. "*I* see ghosts all the time. I've even seen the ghost at that school." With that, Cat leaps into the Deerbergs' yard and scampers away.

"DO YOU THINK HE'S TELLING THE TRUTH?" Mouse asks me. "COULD THERE BE GHOSTS? DO YOU THINK CATS

CAN SEE GHOSTS?"

"I don't know," I say.

A dog can tell when a human is lying, but with cats you never know.

Cats are into some pretty weird things. It's *possible* they see ghosts.

It's also possible Cat with No Name made the whole thing up.

7
It's Hard to Talk to Humans

I need to talk to Jillian. I need to
find a way to ask her what she was
doing in the art room. And I need to
make her understand what I'm asking
so she can answer me.

I don't think a ghost pulled the fire
alarm. Even if there are such things
as ghosts, how would a ghost do it?
And I still don't think Jillian did it,
either. If I can prove she didn't, maybe

Mouse will agree that it's *possible* Michael did it. Then maybe he'll help me prove it.

But how am I going to talk to Jillian? I could probably find her if I went looking for her, but I'm not supposed to wander around the school by myself. I'm supposed to stay here in Mom's office and be a Good Dog.

Well... I don't think Mom would mind if I sat up and looked out the window. I see kids playing outside right now, but they are all younger than Jillian.

Hey, maybe Jillian will come outside in a little bit. When she does, maybe Mom will let me go out and talk to her.

I sit. And I watch as one group of kids comes inside and another, older group, goes outside.

There's Jillian! Over by the swings.

I paw at Mom's lap to get her attention. "Can I go outside?" I beg. "Please, can I go outside?"

Mom looks up from her computer. "Do you need to go outside, Buddy?"

"Yes!" I say, wagging my tail.

Mom snaps my leash to my collar, then takes me outside.

I see Jillian playing by the swings.

"This way," I say, pulling Mom toward Jillian.

"Hey, look! It's Buddy!" "Can Buddy play with us?" "Can Buddy be off the leash?" a group of kids call.

"He can if someone will bring him in after recess," Mom says.

"I will, Mom," Connor says.

"Okay," Mom says, unhooking my leash.

I zoom past all those other kids.

"Hey, Jillian," I say, skidding to a stop in front of her.

"Hi, Buddy," she says. She reaches out to scratch my ears, and I move closer so she can reach. She's really good at scratching ears.

"So, Jillian," I say, "Remember when the fire alarm went off? You were outside talking to one of your friends. You said 'no one saw me.' What did you mean by that? What did you do that no one saw?"

Jillian doesn't understand. "What?

You want to play chase?" Jillian asks.

Chase? I LOVE chase. It's my favorite—NO! I don't want to play chase. "I want you to tell me what you were doing that no one saw. I know you were lying when you told Mom you weren't in the art room. Why did you lie about that?"

"Come on, Buddy." Jillian claps her hands. "Let's go." She runs away from me.

"No," I say, hurrying after her. "I don't want to play chase. I want to talk."

Jillian giggles as she glances back at me, then runs even faster.

But I'm faster than she is. I run in front of her to get her to stop, but she keeps changing direction.

I can't tell if she's doing this on purpose or if she really doesn't understand what I'm saying to her. I know it's hard for humans to understand us, but most of the time if they'd only try—

A bell rings then, and all the kids run toward the school.

"See you later, Buddy," Jillian says with a wave.

I just stand there with my tail hanging heavy. I am no closer to finding out what Jillian was doing when the fire alarm went off than I was before.

"It's frustrating, isn't it?" says a voice behind me.

I turn. It's Jazzy.

"Communicating with humans,

I mean," Jazzy says. "It's frustrating."

"Sure is," I say, making my way toward the fence.

"I was trying to tell my humans about some strange things I saw last night, but they thought I wanted to go outside," Jazzy says.

Strange things? "What strange things?" I ask.

"I saw lights turning on and off in the school," Jazzy says. "Then I saw a girl's face in one of the windows. Except I don't think it was a real girl. I think it was a *ghost* girl."

I stare at Jazzy. "A ghost girl?"

"Yes."

"Was her face burned?" I ask.

"I don't know," Jazzy says. "She was too far away. I couldn't see her very well."

I wasn't sure I believed Cat with No Name when he said he's seen a ghost at this school. But I have to believe Jazzy when she says it because dogs don't lie.

Is it possible that Cat with No Name was telling the truth? Could there be a ghost in the school? Could that ghost have pulled the fire alarm?

8
Missing!

"Buddy, come!" Connor calls from across the playground. He is holding my leash.

I look around. Connor and I are the only ones left on the playground.

"I have to go," I tell Jazzy. Then I turn tail and run to Connor.

"Good boy," he says, clipping my leash to my collar.

Connor seems like a smart human even though he's not full grown yet. "Do you really believe in ghosts, Connor?" I ask as we walk up the stairs. "Do you think there's a ghost in this school?"

Connor just hums a little tune as though I never said a word.

I don't *think* I smell any ghosts in this hallway. But I don't know what ghosts smell like. Do they even have a scent?

If there is a ghost in this school, there should be clues of some sort. If I can't smell it, I should be able to see it. Or hear it.

I stop walking and listen really, really hard. When I listen this hard, I hear things I don't normally hear: balls bouncing … a toilet flushing … water dripping … dishes banging … desks opening and closing … people talking … lots and lots of people talking.

But no ghosts.

"What's the matter, Buddy?" Connor asks.

"Nothing," I say. We continue down the hall, all the way to the office.

Connor unclips my leash and I dash into Mom's office. Hey, Jillian is here, too!

"What are you doing here?" I ask. I go over to her and she pets me.

"Thanks for bringing Buddy in, Connor," Mom says. She motions for Connor to close the door on his way out, then turns back to Jillian.

"I don't know," Mom says. She has a very serious look on her face. "I have to know why you were in the art room before I can promise I won't tell anyone that you were there."

Jillian shifts in her seat. "Okay," she says. "Yesterday was Mrs. Sobol's birthday. Kaity and I decided to give her this pot we made together in our Saturday art class. But we didn't want her or anyone else to know it was from us. We wrote a note that said the pot was from a secret admirer."

"And you snuck it into the art room when you were supposed to be going to the bathroom?" Mom asks.

Jillian nods.

"She's telling the truth!" I tell Mom. I *know* Jillian is telling the truth. I can smell it and I can see it. That means she didn't pull the fire alarm!

So, if Zack didn't pull it, and Jillian didn't pull it, that only leaves Michael. *Or a ghost.*

While I'm thinking about that, I hear footsteps in the hallway. But they're not walking footsteps, they're *running* footsteps!

The door to Mom's office bangs open, and Mrs. Argus rushes in. "You've got to help me!" she cries. "One of my students is missing!"

Mom stands up. "What do you mean one of your students is missing?" she asks.

"It's Zack Goodman," Mrs. Argus says. "He signed out to go to the bathroom, but he never came back. I just took the rest of my class to music, and I checked the bathroom on my way back. He's not in there. I don't know where he could be."

Zack is missing?

"Don't worry. We'll find him," Mom says. "Show me which bathroom you checked."

Mom doesn't tell me to stay, so I get up and follow her and Mrs. Argus down the hall. I pick up a lot of different scents, but none of them are Zack's.

We round a corner and Mrs. Argus says, "This is the bathroom he should have gone to when he signed out."

Mom knocks on the door. "Hello?" she calls. "Is anyone in there?"

We walk in. There's no one in here.

I sniff the stalls, the floor, the sink. I don't think Zack has been here at all today.

"Have you checked the other bathrooms in the school?" Mom asks Mrs. Argus.

"I checked the other one on this floor, but I didn't check the ones upstairs or downstairs," Mrs. Argus says.

"Let's check those, too," Mom says.

I walk with her and Mrs. Argus to the stairs. Mom and Mrs. Argus turn to go up, but I smell something in the other direction. I think it could be Zack.

"Let's go this way," I tell Mom.

"This way, Buddy," Mom calls me.

"No, *this* way," I insist. I start down the stairs.

"I thought you said this dog wasn't going to be running around loose anymore," Mrs. Argus says. "We don't have time to worry about your dog. We have to find Zack!"

"I think maybe Buddy knows something we don't," Mom says. "Let's see where he wants to go."

Mom follows me down the stairs. Mrs. Argus sighs and follows Mom. But I can tell by the sound of her footsteps that she's not happy about it.

"I'm pretty sure this is Zack's scent I'm picking up," I tell them over my shoulder.

Now I'm in the basement.

All that's down here is an empty gymnasium and a wall of storage closets.

The scent ends at the closets. Hmm. I'm confused.

I smell basketballs, soccer balls, and jump ropes. But I also smell Zack!

There's pounding coming from inside the middle closet. And a voice: "Let me out! Let me out!"

9
What Happened to Zack?

"Good boy, Buddy," Mom says, patting my side.

Mrs. Argus bends down in front of the closet. "Zack?" she says to the closed door, "is that you?"

"Yes," a small voice replies.

I scratch at the door, but it doesn't open.

Mom goes into the gym and picks up a phone on the wall. "Would you send Mr. Poe to the storage closets outside the gym, please?" she says into the phone. "Tell him to bring his keys."

We wait a little while, and then I see the man who smells like cleaning stuff lumbering down the stairs. It's the same man who wouldn't let anyone back inside the school when the fire alarm went off.

"What's going on?" the man asks Mom and Mrs. Argus. This must be Mr. Poe.

"One of my first-graders is locked inside this closet," Mrs. Argus says, wringing her hands together.

Mr. Poe frowns at the closet. "How did that happen?" he asks.

Well, there's a lock on the outside of the closet, so I don't think Zack locked himself in there. *Someone else must have locked him in.*

But who would do such a thing? And why? Whoever it was, I bet it was a human, not a ghost.

Mr. Poe pulls a large key ring out of his pocket. He sorts through the keys, then sticks one inside the lock on the closet.

The door swings open. And there, stuffed inside the closet with jump ropes, orange cones, and dirty balls, is Zack.

"Oh, my," Mrs. Argus says as she helps Zack out of the closet and closes the door.

Zack's cheeks are red, and his hair is damp. Water dribbles down his cheeks.

"How did you end up inside the storage closet, Zack?" Mom asks in a soft voice.

Zack sniffs. He doesn't answer.

"Thank you for unlocking the closet," Mom says to Mr. Poe. Then she turns to Zack and Mrs. Argus. "I know you have to get back to your class, Mrs. Argus. But Zack? I'd like you to come to my office. We'll get you cleaned up and get you a drink of water. Then maybe we can talk about what happened."

Zack swallows hard. I don't think he wants to talk about what happened.

"I'm glad we found you, Zack," Mrs. Argus says, patting his back. "I was worried about you." She glances at me, and I think she might even pet me. Or at least tell me I'm a good dog. But she just turns and walks away.

Oh, well.

Mr. Poe closes the closet. Mom, Zack, and Mrs. Argus all head back upstairs.

I sniff around the outside of the closet. Besides Zack's scent, I smell bananas, sweat socks, pencils, dirt, hamburger—wait a minute! I think the bananas, sweat socks, and dirt scent belongs to one person. And the hamburger, pencils, and dirt scent belongs to a different person.

I've smelled these people before. Where?

"Come on, Buddy," Mom calls from the other end of the hallway.

"I'm coming," I say, hurrying to catch up with Mom and Zack.

It's just us in Mom's office. Mom, Zack, and me.

Mom sits beside Zack rather than at her desk. "Who locked you in that closet, Zack?" she asks softly.

Zack just stares at his feet.

"Are you afraid to tell me?" Mom asks.

Again no answer.

"Yes," I tell Mom with my eyes. "He's *very* afraid." I can smell the fear all over him. In fact, that's why I'm talking to Mom with my eyes instead of my mouth. This boy is so scared that I'm afraid to talk with my mouth.

I go over to him and lick his hand. *What are you so afraid of? You can tell Mom who locked you in that closet.*

"Is someone at school giving you a hard time?" Mom asks.

Zack still doesn't answer, but I watch the way his mouth twitches. "I think the answer is yes," I tell Mom.

"Are you afraid that if you tell me who's giving you a hard time, things will only get worse for you?" Mom asks.

Zack's bottom lip twitches again. "That's another yes," I tell Mom.

Mom sighs. "I can't help you if you won't talk to me, honey," she says.

He may not be talking with his mouth, but he's still talking. And I'm *trying* to translate for Mom. She's just not getting the message.

What else could I do to help? I could go into all the classrooms and sniff around. Eventually, I'd find the kid who smells like bananas, sweat socks, and dirt. And the kid who smells like hamburger, pencils, and dirt.

But I'm not supposed to wander around the school. I'm supposed to stay in Mom's office. Can I figure out who locked Zack in the closet without leaving Mom's office? I don't know.

I wish I could remember where else I've smelled those scents before. I think and I think and I think ... but it's not coming to me.

Maybe it would help to make a list of things I know and things I don't know about the Case of the Kid in the Closet.

Here is what I know:

- 🐾 Zack left his classroom to go to the bathroom.
- 🐾 Someone has been giving Zack a hard time.
- 🐾 Somebody—more than one somebody—locked him in the storage closet.
- 🐾 Zack knows who did it.
- 🐾 Zack is afraid to tell who did it.
- 🐾 Zack is afraid that whoever locked him in the closet will do something even worse if he tells.

Here is what I don't know:

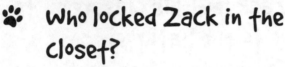

😾 Who has been giving Zack
a hard time?
😾 Who locked Zack in the
closet?

Here is my plan:
???

I lie down and think about this.
Zack won't talk because he's
scared. He was awfully scared when
he was talking to Mom about the
fire drill, too. Why? *Maybe he saw
who pulled the alarm.*

Maybe the person who pulled the
alarm knows that Zack saw him and
is afraid Zack is going to tell. So he

locked Zack in the storage closet to
warn him to keep quiet.

I hop up and nudge Zack's arm to
get his attention. "Did you see who
pulled the fire alarm?" I ask. "Was it
Michael?"

He doesn't answer.

"Mom!" I say. "Ask Zack if he saw
who pulled the fire alarm! I think the
person who pulled the fire alarm is
the same person who locked Zack in
the storage closet."

"Buddy, do you have to go outside?"
Mom asks.

"NO!" I say. Why do humans
always think we have to go outside?

"I can take him outside, Mrs. K.,"
says a kid I don't know. He's about
Zack's age, and he's sort of bouncing

around in Mom's doorway. He's like a little human pogo stick...jumping, jumping, jumping.

"*I'll* take Buddy outside," Ellie says from the other office. "Why don't you sit down, Tristan. Mrs. Keene isn't ready to talk to you yet."

But instead of sitting down, Tristan leaps up and slaps the top of the doorjamb.

Wow! That kid can jump *high!*

"Sit down, Tristan!" Ellie says, leading him to a bench beside her desk. "Save your jumping for the playground."

"I don't think Buddy needs to go outside," Mom says. She reaches over and closes the door.

She probably said that because

she wanted Ellie to stay in the office and keep an eye on that human jumping bean.

Hey, wait a minute. *Human jumping bean?*

That gives me a whole new idea about who might have pulled the fire alarm. *And* who locked Zack inside the storage closet.

10
Who Pulled the Fire Alarm?

I remember now where I smelled the bananas, sweat socks, and dirt scent. And the hamburger, pencils, and dirt scent. Those scents belonged to the kids who were in that club, the Sharks. They told Zack he had to do something no one else in the school had ever done if he wanted to get into the club. Has anyone else in this school ever pulled a fire alarm?

I go over to Zack and lay my

head in his lap. "Did *you* pull the fire alarm, Zack?" I ask with my eyes.

I know he can jump really high. I saw him on the playground. He jumped to a really high bar on the climbing toy. Could he reach the alarm if he *jumped*?

"Are those boys afraid you'll tell Mom that it's their fault you pulled the alarm?" I ask. "Did they lock you in the storage closet to warn you to keep quiet?"

Zack is looking everywhere except at me.

"You should tell Mom if that's what happened," I say, snuggling deeper into his lap.

"Buddy must like you, Zack," Mom says. "You can pet him, if you want."

"Yeah, you can pet me if you want," I say.

He touches my head. Then pats me gently on the back.

"If you don't want to tell me how you got locked in the storage closet, maybe you can tell Buddy," Mom says. "He's a good listener."

Zack's hand starts to shake a little. I think he *wants* to tell me what happened, but he's afraid.

I lick Zack's hand. "Mom's right. I *am* a good listener."

Zack looks at me. "Some second-graders locked me in the closet," he says in a small voice. "They did it because they didn't want me to tell anyone about their club."

"What club is that?" Mom asks.

Zack swallows. "The Sharks. You have to do something no one else in the whole school has ever done to get in." He pauses. "So I ... pulled the fire alarm."

I knew it!

Mom draws in her breath. "I see," she says, sitting back in her chair. "I'm glad you told Buddy and me."

Zack bites his lip. "Am I going to go to jail?"

"No," Mom says. "But I am going to call your parents. And I'll need the names of the other kids who are in the Sharks, too. We need to talk about the difference between a good club and a bad club."

Mom moves my pillow out of her office and sets it next to Ellie's desk. "Lie down, Buddy," she says, pointing to the pillow.

I lie down. "What's going on?" I say.

But Mom and Ellie are too busy moving chairs from Ellie's office into Mom's office to answer me.

Mrs. Argus, the kids from the Sharks, and some parents come in. They go into Mom's office and Mom closes the door. Ellie gives my head a pat, then turns to her computer.

A bell rings. Kids pour into the hallway and I hear talking and laughing. Then it is quiet.

Mom's door remains closed.

After a while, Ellie turns off her

computer. She knocks lightly on Mom's door. "I'm heading out, Sarah," she says to the closed door. "Buddy is sleeping on his pillow. Would you like me to bring him in there with you, or do you think he's okay out here?"

"He's fine out there," Mom says. "I'll see you tomorrow, Ellie. Thanks."

"See you tomorrow," Ellie replies. "And I'll see you tomorrow, too, Buddy." She reaches into her pocket and tosses me a liver treat. I LOVE liver treats. They're my favorite food! Ellie smiles, then turns out the light in the main office and leaves.

I put my head back down on my paws and close my eyes. Now that I've solved the Case of the Fire Alarm and the Case of the Kid in the Cabinet,

maybe I can give up detective work
once and for all.

I'm thinking happy thoughts
as I drift off to sleep. Nothing but
happy thoughts. Liver treats…
cheese…bacon and eggs…

All of a sudden I have the
strangest feeling I'm being watched.

My eyes pop open. I don't see
anything. But I feel a cool burst of air
ripple through my fur. I shiver.
Then the office door slams shut.

I leap to my feet. The windows
aren't open. And there's no one here
who could have closed that door.

The door to Mom's office opens.
"What was that noise?" she asks.
She glances toward the closed office
door. "Oh, Mr. Poe must've come and

closed that door."

Mr. Poe? No, I don't think so. I didn't see him, and I didn't smell him.

I think back to what Jazzy told me about seeing strange things in the school during the night. I remember what Connor told Michael about the school being haunted. And what Cat with No Name said: *I've seen the ghost at the school.*

Could there be a ghost here?

Hmm ... maybe I shouldn't give up the detective business just yet. I have a feeling there are more cases to solve around this school. Besides, I LOVE being a detective. It's my favorite thing!

The Buddy Files

Have you read all of Buddy's mysteries?

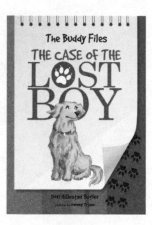

THE BUDDY FILES:
THE CASE OF THE LOST BOY

King has a very big mystery to solve. His family is missing, and he's been put in the P-o-U-N-D. Why doesn't his beloved human (Kayla) come to get him? When King is adopted by Connor and his mom, things get more confusing. The new family calls him Buddy! And just as Connor and Buddy start to get acquainted, Connor disappears! With some help from his friend Mouse (a very large dog) and the mysterious Cat with No Name, Buddy shows what a smart, brave dog can do.

HC 978-0-8075-0910-4 • $14.99
PB 978-0-8075-0932-6 • $4.99

THE BUDDY FILES: THE CASE OF THE MIXED-UP MUTTS

Buddy was adopted from the P-o-U-N-D and he likes his new family, but he's still searching for Kayla and her dad—his first family. What has happened to them? He hopes to solve that mystery soon, but right now he's got another urgent case—two dogs, Muffin and Jazzy, have been switched! How can Buddy get poor Muffin and Jazzy back to their real owners?
HC 978-0-8075-0911-1 • $14.99
PB 978-0-8075-0933-3 • $4.99

THE BUDDY FILES: THE CASE OF THE MISSING FAMILY

Buddy has settled in with his adopted family, but he's never given up on finding his beloved human, Kayla, and his first family. One night he sees people taking things out of Kayla's old house and loading them into a van. What's up? Though his friend Mouse advises against it, in the middle of the night Buddy decides to make a daring move, leaving everything he knows behind. Dori Butler's third case in *The Buddy Files* will entertain and satisfy the many fans of this brave, funny, and loyal dog.
HC 978-0-8075-0912-8 • $14.99
PB 978-0-8075-0934-0 • $4.99

Praise for The Buddy Files

"With twists and turns, humor, and a likable canine character, this series should find a wide fan base."—*Booklist*

"Readers should be drawn in by Buddy's exuberant voice."
—*Publishers Weekly*

"Sweet and suspenseful."
—*Kirkus Reviews*

The Buddy Files

Have you read all of Buddy's mysteries?

Turn the page and see!

#1

The Buddy Files

THE CASE OF THE
LOST BOY

Dori Hillestad Butter

THE BUDDY FILES:
THE CASE OF THE LOST BOY

King has a very big mystery to solve.
His family is missing, and he's been
put in the **P-o-U-n-D**. Why doesn't
his beloved human (Kayla) come
to get him? When King is adopted
by Connor and his mom, things get
more confusing. The new family calls
him Buddy! And just as Connor and
Buddy start to get acquainted, Connor
disappears! With some help from his
friend Mouse (a very large dog) and
the mysterious Cat with No Name,
Buddy shows what a smart, brave dog
can do.
HC 978-0-8075-0910-4 • $14.99
PB 978-0-8075-0932-6 • $4.99

#2

The Buddy Files

THE CASE OF THE MIXED-UP MUTTS

Dori Hillestad Butler

Pictures by Jeremy Tugeau

THE BUDDY FILES: THE CASE OF THE MIXED-UP MUTTS

Buddy was adopted from the P-o-U-N-D and he likes his new family, but he's still searching for Kayla and her dad—his first family. What has happened to them? He hopes to solve that mystery soon, but right now he's got another urgent case—two dogs, Muffin and Jazzy, have been switched! How can Buddy get poor Muffin and Jazzy back to their real owners?
HC 978-0-8075-0911-1 • $14.99
PB 978-0-8075-0933-3 • $4.99

#3

The Buddy Files

THE CASE OF THE MISSING FAMILY

Dori Hillestad Butler

THE BUDDY FILES: THE CASE OF THE MISSING FAMILY

Buddy has settled in with his adopted family, but he's never given up on finding his beloved human, Kayla, and his first family. One night he sees people taking things out of Kayla's old house and loading them into a van. What's up? Though his friend Mouse advises against it, in the middle of the night Buddy decides to make a daring move, leaving everything he knows behind. Dori Butler's third case in *The Buddy Files* will entertain and satisfy the many fans of this brave, funny, and loyal dog.
HC 978-0-8075-0912-8 • $14.99
PB 978-0-8075-0934-0 • $4.99

#4

THE BUDDY FILES: THE CASE OF THE FIRE ALARM

Buddy is starting his work as a therapy dog at Four Lakes Elementary School, where Connor attends and Mom is the principal. On his very first day, he accidentally knocks down a little kid on the playground, convincing the first grade teacher that school is no place for a dog. Then the fire alarm goes off. The school is evacuated, but there's no fire...it's a false alarm. Who could have set it?
HC 978-0-8075-0913-5 • $14.99
PB 978-0-8075-0935-7 • $4.99

#5

The Buddy Files

THE CASE OF THE
LIBRARY
MONSTER

Dori Hillestad Butler
Pictures by Jeremy Tugeau

THE BUDDY FILES: THE CASE OF THE LIBRARY MONSTER

One of Buddy's jobs as a therapy dog is to read books with the kids in the school library! One day he hears a noise in the bookshelves. He tries to get closer—and comes face to face with a creature that has a blue tongue! What is it? And how did it get in the school?
HC 978-0-8075-0914-2 • $14.99